THE TALE OF TROUT & BEAR

Dedicated to bears, dogs, pigs, rabbits, foxes, mice beavers, anteaters &, of course, trout ~ you all know who you are.

xxx

Written & Illustrated by
Jacqui Taylor

Once upon a time,
not so very long ago,
there was a trout
who lived in a beautiful river
that ran through a green valley
deep in the mountains.

She was a rainbow trout who spent much of her time
dreaming of impossible things.

Like having wings.
(On a fish? Imagine that!
But she did.)

As a result of her dreaming, she was always swimming
into rocks or getting tangled in tree roots that reached
deep into the riverbed.
Or falling carelessly down waterfalls.

Her family and friends fretted about her terribly.
They were always trying to guide her out of danger and
whispered worried words among themselves such as,
"One day she will be eaten if she's not careful!"
She nevertheless persisted in her aimless
dreaming (and bumping into, getting stuck in
and falling down things).

Deep in the tall trees
that lined the banks of the river,
there lived a bear.

He was large, solitary and fairly grumpy, as bears go.
He did have a sense of humour but kept mislaying it
somewhere or other and only stumbled on it
occasionally and when he was least expecting it.
Bear believed that most creatures were really not
very intelligent and therefore not worth engaging
in conversation. He was a bear of very few words.

As a bear of great reason and not much imagination,
also, he mostly lived on a steady diet of roots
and berries (especially goji berries,
his favourite), honey if he could find it,
and the occasional fish.

On no particular morning, on waking, his big bear brain would reason
that it was time to go fishing. And he did. Shambling down the
mountainside through the tall trees, he would survey his beardom and
sniff the air. Arriving at the riverbank, he would stand very still,
all four bear paws planted solidly, and stare into
the shimmering blue of the rushing river. Looking for fish.

One particularly pleasant June morning, he was doing just this.
Imagine his surprise when he saw, right below him, where his nose
almost touched the water, the face of a fish
looking straight back up at him.

He was mightily astonished, for most fish swim as fast and as far away
from bears as they can. Lickety split! This must be his lucky day - to have
(what appeared to be) a magnificently gullible catch right under his nose
and there for the taking. However, his reason said,
"If something looks too good to be true, it most certainly is."
As a result of Bear's inner conflict and Trout's blissful oblivion,
they stared into each other's amber eyes for a very long moment.

What was Trout thinking? She was thinking, "This bear is covered with an
awful lot of hair; I wonder how long it would take to count them all?"
But she was still not unduly worried.

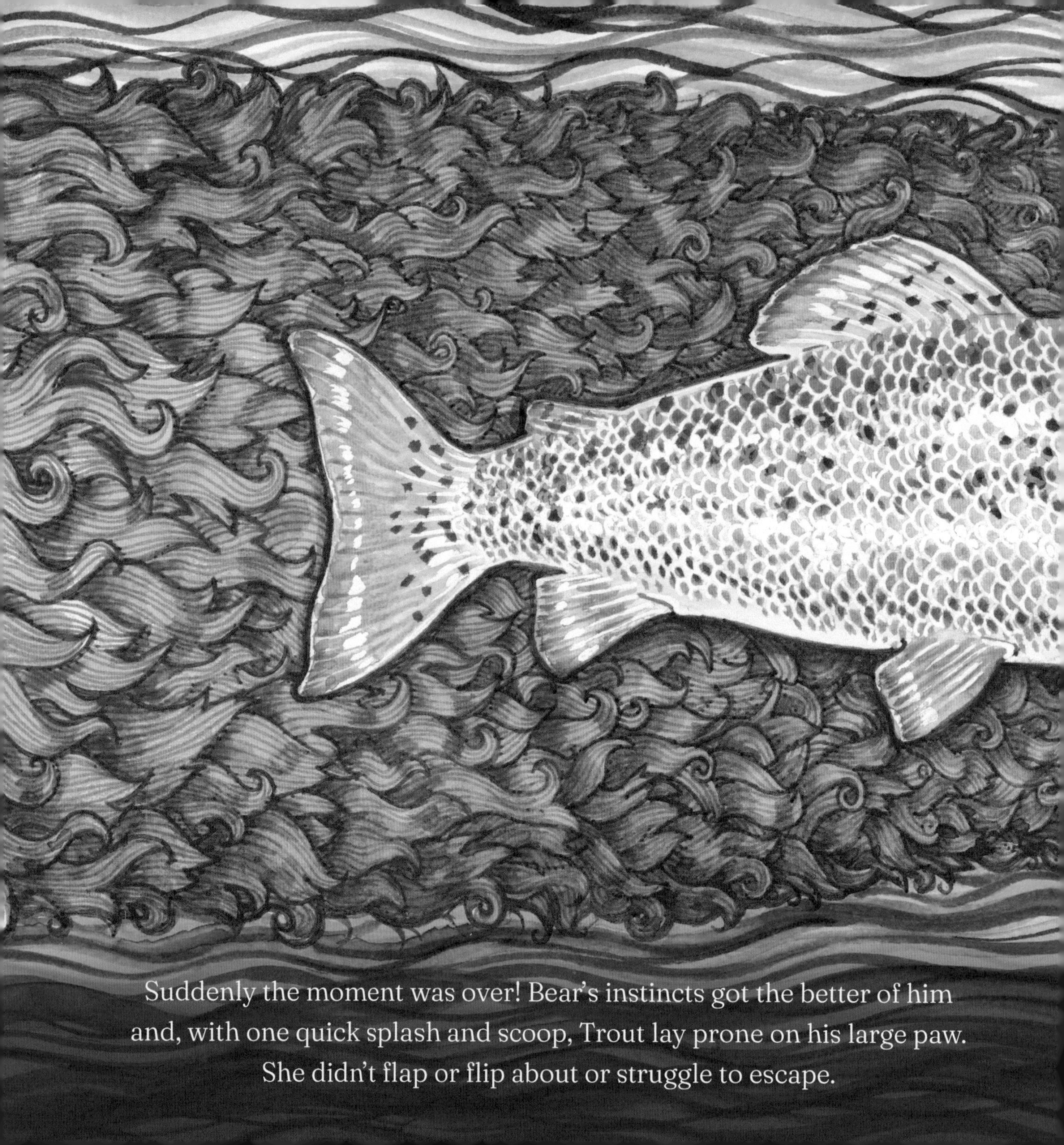

Suddenly the moment was over! Bear's instincts got the better of him and, with one quick splash and scoop, Trout lay prone on his large paw. She didn't flap or flip about or struggle to escape.

She just lay there quietly, with her mouth opening and closing gently
as she whispered, "Put me back please,
I can't breathe very well out here where you are."

Bear was flabbergasted! He had always assumed
that fish were far too stupid to speak.
He looked into her perfectly circular, bright eye
and at the shimmering rainbow of her scales in the sun.
And his big bear brain told him,
"This is not just a fish.
This is a slippery, little slice of mercurial magic."

Bear simply could not bring himself to have her for luncheon, so
he lowered her gently back into the water and let her swim away.
And she loved Bear for that. Some part of her dreamy, drifting brain
told her that he had spared her.

From that day on, Bear came to the river almost daily. Trout swam
beside him as he splashed in the shallows and told him stories
and flashed reflections at him of all the beauty in her universe.
They coloured his solitary bear dreams. And he loved Trout for that.

He walked next to her in the river
and stopped her from falling down waterfalls
or being eaten alive.

He began, ever so slowly, to share
his bear wisdom with her (this took a while,
he being a bear of few words).

Over the summer they shared a thousand stories.
Bear would lie under the moon late into
the warm nights, his paw trailing in the water,
listening to Trout's low, soft voice.

In the day he would wade up the river with Trout swimming lazy circles around him, while he told her stories of meadows and flowers and butterflies that landed on his nose.

When the leaves began to change colour and, one by one,
drifted down to earth, Bear was visited by a creeping sorrow.
For he knew that the winter was coming and that they would be
separated by long months of ice and snow. He knew that bears
must hibernate and store their energy to get through the winter.
And that fish, even magic trout, must snuggle down into the mud
of the river bed and sleep until spring.

Trout saw Bear's sadness and confessed tearfully,
"I wish I had wings! Then I could fly with you
into the forest and see your life
and be with you, sometimes."
Bear shook his head and answered quietly,
"That would never work, dear Trout."

The day the first snow fell
and ice started to form at the edges of the river,
they said goodbye.

Trout wept into the river
as she watched Bear disappear into the forest
with his shoulders and his head hung low.

Then she turned, with pain in her heart, and swam down,
down in to the mud to sleep.

Bear's deep winter dreams were punctuated with flying fish and rainbows.
Trout's frosty dreams were of soaring through the forest
beside her beloved Bear.

The long months passed, the river lay frozen
and the valley slept, blanketed in snow.

But all things change with time.

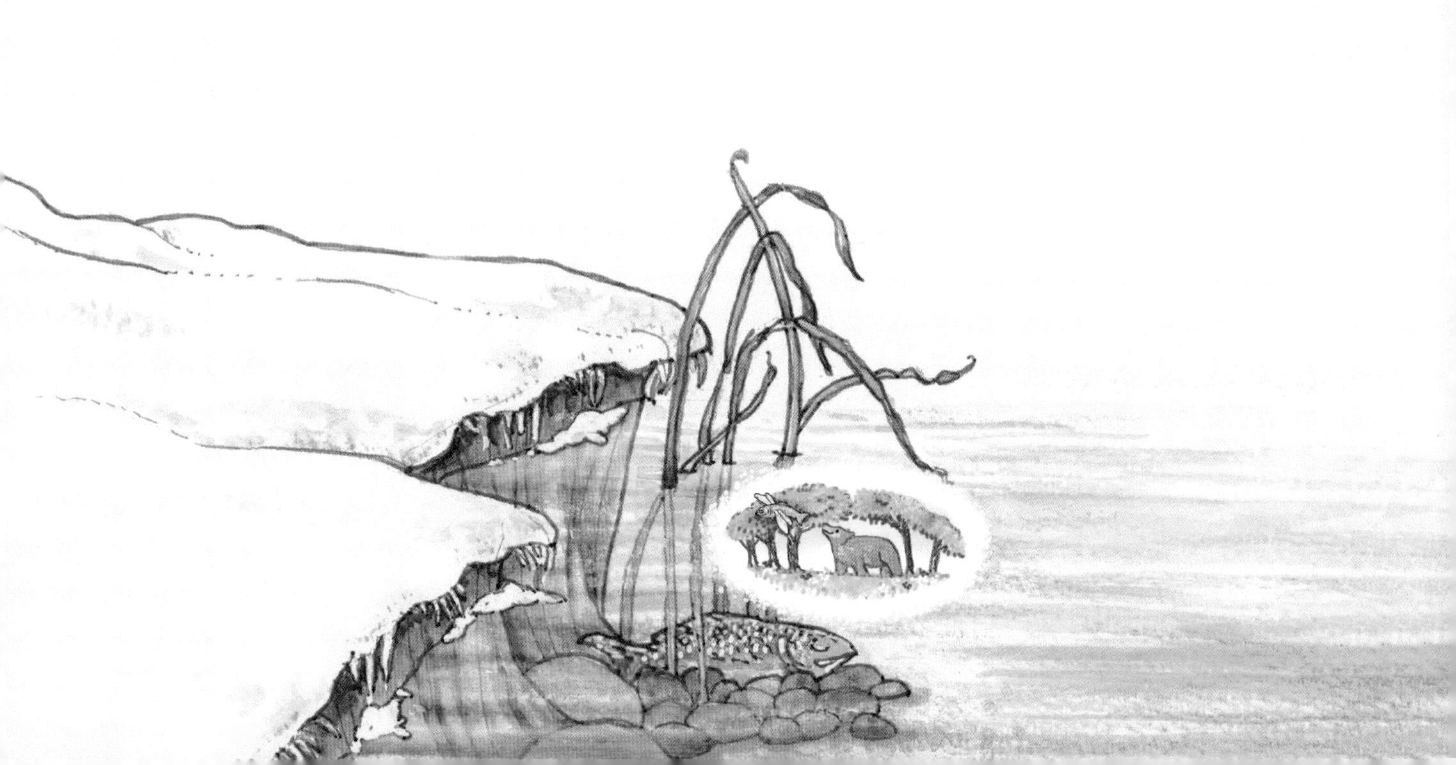

Bear stirred as the snow began to melt.
He awoke, stretching and grumbling with pins and needles
in his left back paw and a loudly grumbling belly.
He awoke thinking, "There must be a way".

Going out from his cave, he heard the birds singing again and
the water flowing down to the river as the ice melted.
He foraged furiously for new shoots and roots and had a very large
and satisfying vegetarian bear-breakfast.

As he was foraging, he came upon a pile of rubbish. Those exceptionally annoying human animals had dumped a whole pile of unwanted stuff at the edge of the forest near the road. Bear shook his head in disgust. Humans were surely the most stupid animal of all!

Bear then mused for a moment. “Hold on a minute!” he thought, “I may be able to do something with this lot.” Bear had always harboured a secret desire to become an engineer. He had read about it, studied it extensively if truth be known; the only thing precluding him from becoming one was the fact that he was a bear!

Now he would put his rich knowledge to
good use. For the next day or so, Bear pushed,
pulled, manipulated and created a contraption that
Heath Robinson would have been proud of.
(If you don't know who he is, Google him!)

Once this fabulous construction was complete
and in place, Bear hastened to the river to wait for Trout.

He lay on the riverbank for two days at the place
they usually met, wondering if he'd missed her,
hoping she would remember him, only crawling
back into the warmth of his cave at night
after scrabbling for a few juicy roots
to keep him going.

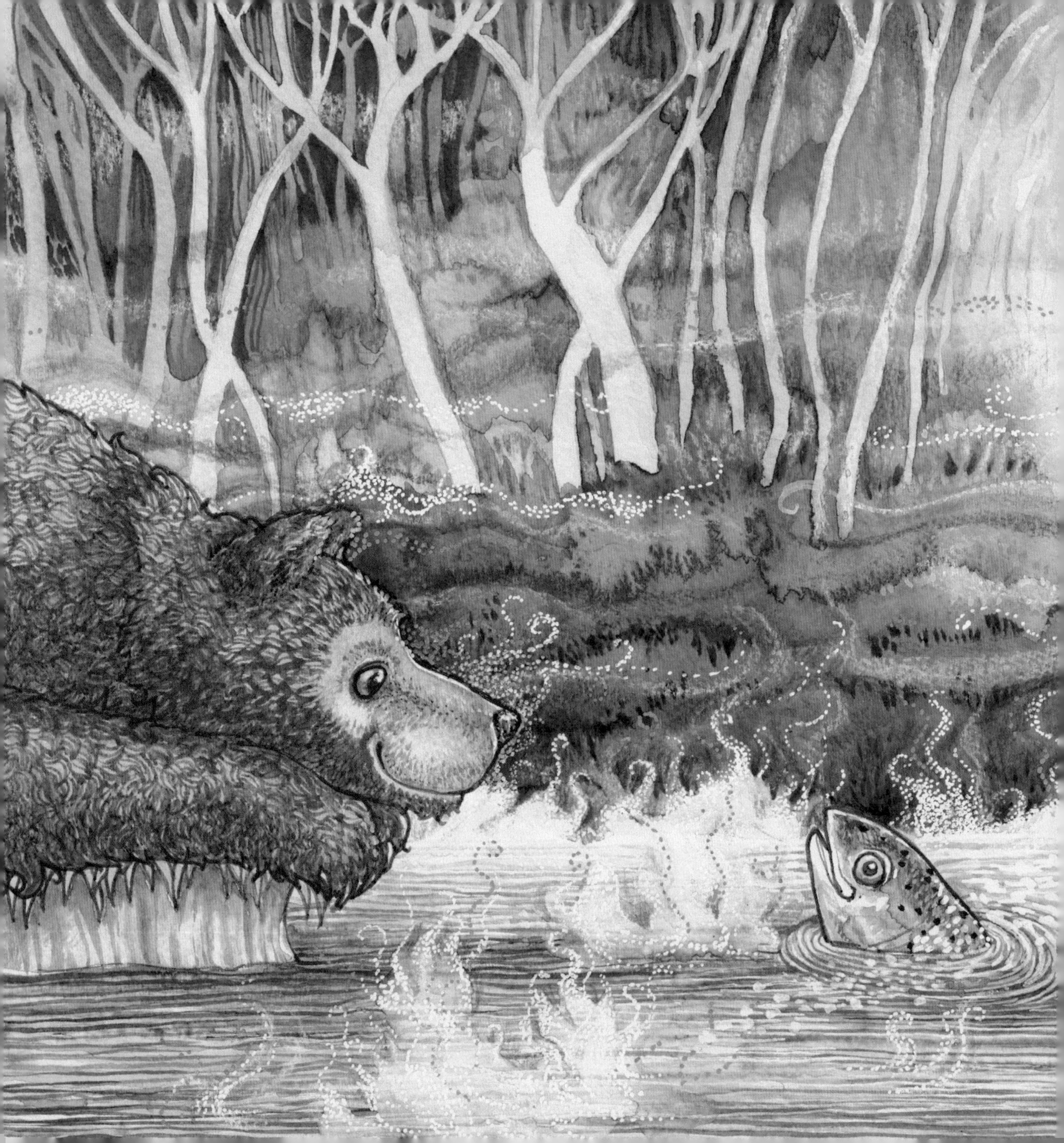

Early on the third day,
as Bear began his vigil, through the mist
on the water rose a slim, silvery head and an amber eye.
It was, indeed, his dear Trout.

After their initial delight in reunion, Trout's eyes
grew wider and wider (if that is at all possible for a fish)
at the sight of the contraption attached to Bear.

Awestruck, she asked, "What on earth is that, Bear?"

"I made it so you can fly to visit
my world, sometimes, Trout," he replied shyly.
"It may not be wings, but I think it will do the trick."

You may be wondering what Bear had built
and, quite frankly, there are no words...

... just use your imagination.

Trout and Bear continue to visit each other's worlds,
living as happily-ever-after as can be.

....

After visiting the worlds of Trout and Bear,
these are the messages they hope your heart has heard.

Try to look upon everything that life brings you as a chance to learn.

....

Love can be found in the places we least expect.

•

Not all creatures are the same - celebrate the differences.

•

Use what is at your disposal to build something beautiful or useful
- preferably both.

•

Be patient with your dreams and hopes
- some things take longer than others.

•

Be like Bear - think carefully about what you eat before you eat it.

•

Be like Trout - never stop dreaming.

www.jacquitaylor.com

Printed in Poland
by Amazon Fulfillment
Poland Sp. z o.o., Wrocław